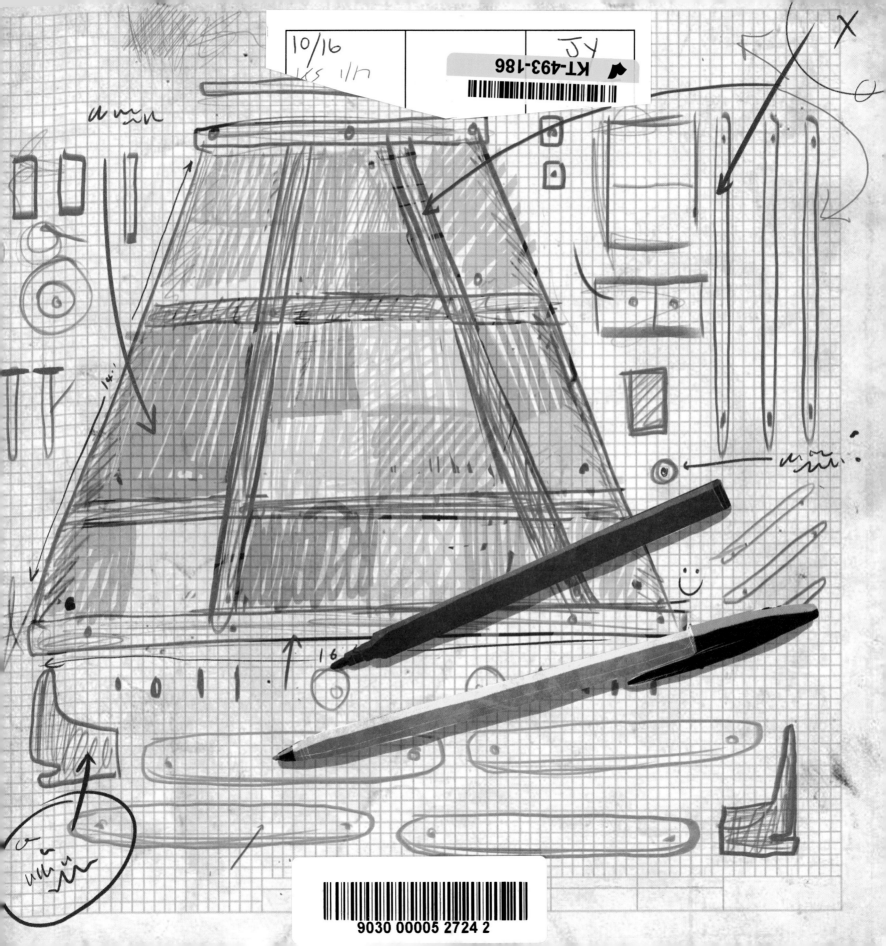

The
BUILDING
BOY

R. M – For Joe

D. L – For Katie and Ben

First published in the UK in 2016
by Faber and Faber Limited
Bloomsbury House,
74–77 Great Russell Street, London WC1B 3DA

HB ISBN 978–0–571–31409–6
PB ISBN 978–0–571–31410–2

➤ A FABER PICTURE BOOK ◄

The BUILDING BOY

ff

FABER & FABER

Each night before the boy went to bed,
he would light the fire.
He would squeeze beside Grandma on her favourite chair.
The house would be quiet, except for the turning of a page
and the ticking of a clock.

And Grandma would show
the boy her photographs.

Grandma had been an architect. She made the tallest skyscrapers, the most beautiful palaces, and museums and libraries bigger than towns. But they would be nothing, she said, compared to the house she would build for the boy.

The house would sit on the hill that lay on the horizon, over the city and beyond the sea.

"When will we move there, Grandma?" the boy would ask. Grandma would just nod her head and say, "Soon."

But Grandma was getting old – too old to make houses.

Soon she was too old to make dinner, and then she was too old to climb the stairs.

One day she was too old to sit up in bed, and by the time the boy came home, she was gone.

Without Grandma, the house was empty.
It was just rooms.

But the boy had an idea.

He made his plans
and he set to work.

The boy worked

through wind

and snow

and rain.

And when the work was done,
the boy looked into the eyes he
had built himself and said,

"Grandma, wake up."

All at once it was as if the stars leapt closer.

With one swipe of her giant hands, Grandma grabbed the
boy, raising him high above the roof tiles on her head.

She was alive!

"Grandma?' the boy gasped.

"Is it really you?"

Without warning, Grandma leapt into the air.
She cleared six gardens in a single bound.

"Stop!" the boy cried.

"Where are you taking me?"

They flew at a sprint over moonlit fields, leaping over hedges, scattering the hares.

The boy's lungs throbbed with the cold night air, and his ears rang with the clang of Grandma's great metal feet on the stony ground.

"Where are you taking me?" he cried again.

They came to the sea.
It stretched out before them,
still as a sheet.

Grandma ploughed into the waves.

For hours they walked the great wide ocean.

Mackerel circled round Grandma's steel shoulders.

Clouds of ocean sand billowed beneath her with every step.

Starfish caked her metal ribs like the hull of a sunken ship.

Soon, a city rose out of the water.
Grandma flung herself straight onto the rooftops.
A forest of streetlamps and skyscrapers
flew beneath them.

"Stop!" the boy cried.

But Grandma ran on, until the sounds of the city were lost behind them and there was nothing but the wind on the hills.

"Where are you taking…" the boy began.

Then he saw it.

On the hill above the city that lay beyond
the sea, was the house that Grandma
had built for him.

But the house had never been finished.

It was just bricks and glass and girders.

A great hole lay in the middle of it.

"Welcome home," said Grandma.

"But I can't live here," the boy said.
"It's only half a house, how will I ever finish it?"

Grandma smiled. The boy could suddenly see the
stars through the windows of her eyes.

"You already did," she whispered.